TUESDAY OR SEPTEMBER OR THE END

Hannah Black

for my friends

If someone asked me the date I would look at a mirror, if someone asked me who I was I would want to see a calendar.

-John Edgar Wideman

JANUARY

COMMON TIME

Common Time

It was only January 2020 and already Bird was sick of hearing about the aliens.

She was forced to ingest the news continuously because all the TVs at work were set to CNN. No one was born wanting to pay five hundred dollars to get their hair cut and colored amid the blaring, toony faces of newscasters and a stream of horror images. Although she was pleased by the generous tips, much improved from her last place of work, it seemed to Bird that her customers' choice of salon indicated that something had gone wrong in their lives.

Technically nothing had gone wrong in their lives; they had a lot of money. All that had gone wrong in their lives had also gone wrong in the life of the world.

Bird could do everything, but she specialized in color. She could match any skin tone to its ideal hair shade on sight. She had a gift: it was fun, a trip, to change lives daily with Olaplex and bleach. She believed that her eye had been trained through generations of heavy chromatic meaning para-originating in the Caribbean, where her parents were born, via London, where she was born, to New York City, where she now lived.

Best and worst of all, through her work she was able to perceive movements in the general mood. Since the alien object had appeared in early January, just days after America tried to provoke a war with Iran, customers couldn't talk about anything else. The discovery had been made on Jones Beach. So close!

A Classics professor who insisted on a kind of feathery '90s cut told Bird that the object resembled the oak rods used in the ceremonial prophecies at the ancient Temple of Fortuna while Bird dyed a green ombre into her hair. Sensing Bird's lack of interest, the professor asked if she thought the whole aliens thing was a hoax. Bird didn't think it was a hoax; she just didn't think it was interesting. We had made so little progress as a species in communicating with whales, apes or each other. Humans had underdeveloped the abilities that would have made the moment of alien contact special. Sadly, as usual, there was nothing to get excited about.

Cleaning up after hours, Bird and her colleagues at the salon switched to music videos. The screens were permanently set to the hyper-realistic glaze they put on sportscasts, so everything looked like a panic attack: jumpy, too-vivid, flat.

Clearly, cinema was in the process of being not just technologically but spiritually murdered by the increasingly cinematic quality of everyday life. There was an atmosphere of saturated, narrative repetition in the air that felt like simulation or psychosis. But, when you put feelings aside for a second, it was probably something much more drab, like the slow death of a form of society.

*

The news reported over and over that everyone, every living American, was enraptured by the alien object. There were crowds at Jones Beach and the city had a hectic, anticipatory air, crammed with tourists of all kinds, many who had evidently never been to New York before. Bird felt alone in not caring. She was tired of talking about aliens. She wanted to talk about her feelings. But her boyfriend Dog was among the enraptured many. As a social democrat, he sought to embrace popular feeling. He had gone down to Jones Beach claiming simple curiosity but came back with his mind made up. Just looking at the object had made him believe. Its substance had a strange resonance. It really did look like oak, like the professor had said, but seemed to have been produced by technological methods.

"Another customer said she thought it was alive, but sleeping," said Bird.

Dog's face lit up. "Do you think so?"

"I don't know. You can never talk anyone out of blond, but I don't think she suits any type of it."

"Bird!"

Bird was stubborn and did not want to give herself an interesting encounter with the alien material. She would prefer to continue to be wrong, which did not require her to turn to face her wrongness. So, while the world was raving about and obsessed with the alien object, in Bird and Dog's apartment it was equal parts alien and mundane. It was a rod of unknown material with a pattern on its surface. And the truth was, nothing else was yet known.

Every few hours or days or whatever, Dog raised his head from the glowing window of his phone. The world was the window and hidden inside his body, and his body was lost outside the world. Inside the screen, beyond the window that was also the world, the world was on fire.

What did he think about, as he allowed catastrophe to scroll through him? A pad with notes in his handwriting read *forget it* written compulsively maybe two or three hundred times. And he really had forgotten writing all that—when the subconscious said jump, then the mind that knew its own name asked how high. Metonymic sensations of Bird's presence ran a ladder up the vertiginous edges of the feeling of a broken world: the smell of candy flavored Juuls and rose oil on skin, local talk radio mixed in with the waterfall sound of the shower. Soon she would emerge wet and shining to tell him something new. Without this tether to reality, who knows what could have happened.

The weather stayed bearable, not cold enough—it was freaky, everyone said. Four days a week, Dog went to a call center where he sat for eight to ten hours and listened to strangers cry and rage about their health insurance. At first the job had been weirdly energizing—the extraordinary radiance of the suffering of strangers had electrified him. Now, it was numbing and aggravating at the same time. He believed that it was possible for a person to waste their life, and this bothered him. This conservationist stance on life dried out his personality a little and focused him inward—at least, more than he would have liked, if he could have chosen himself from a menu.

As Dog would later explain to the aliens, to justify why

he had spent so much of the life he believed he could waste making people cry on the phone, once a month the call center deposited money in his bank account. A lot of things could have happened, a lot of forms of social organization, but at this point in history, January 2020, world of dwindling animals, the wage and its dread exterior had achieved insane predominance as an organizing principle. Human life at that point was like a fucked-up car. Some people who understood how it worked could drive it a certain distance, but it would eventually have to be taken to the scrapyard and recycled into something more bearable.

As a result of his call center job, Dog had become passionately interested in the electoral campaign of Moley Salamanders. The elderly senator had taken advantage of a power vacuum opened up by the incredible incompetence and laziness of the Democratic Party to attempt to bring universal healthcare to the USA. While centrist Democrats were still scrambling to regain ground they had lost, either by having shit for brains or through innate malevolence—Dog was not sure which—Moley's campaign had gone from strength to strength, partly thanks to enthusiastic volunteers like Dog.

Since the Jones Beach Incident, Moley's pragmatic, cautiously optimistic stance on aliens had taken the country by storm, propelling him to the head of a wide field of candidates for the Democratic nomination. These included decrepit Shark, raddled Pony, soulless Rat, each candidate apparently vying for who could be the least charismatic. What they had done to defend themselves against having to provide universal healthcare—i.e. make it sound stupid and complicated—they could not do for the arrival of aliens. The aliens were popular across the entire political spectrum because everyone was sick of every person, animal and thing on Earth.

Bird alone continued to be aggressively uninterested in the aliens. She might perhaps have lifted an eyebrow at an alien declaration of war, but then she would have had to die embarrassed. In any case, the alien object remained mute, still awaiting interpretation.

*

Bird had moved to New York from London early in the fake Mayan apocalypse year of 2012. She came straight from the London riots of 2011—the last beautiful thing that ever happened in England—to New York. The world-historical light emanating from the riots' brief recapture of reality was extinguished from general view, but Bird kept a part of it with her. She had learned with her body that riots expressed the collective desire to revolutionize life. As she would later explain to the aliens, revolution was the return of time's living, plant-like cyclicality—if messianic, then the messiah in his pagan aspect of springtime, the part that comes again and again. The world resists its reduction to winter.

She had brought this intuition with her in hope to New York City in the era of President Llama. It was sad to discover that the feeling of formless but certain doom that followed the riots and the repression of the riots in London prevailed for different reasons in New York too. As if time were thread, the future was barred by a knot that could not be untied.

This was all before President Pig murdered the dying language of politics and resurrected it as abstract poetry. Under political pressure, Pig had renounced his initial position that the aliens should be nuked. It was not popular among his base. The aliens' popularity exceeded his. He therefore had two choices: destroy the aliens or fall in love with them. Having failed at the former, he chose the latter. He gave long, rambling speeches describing his love, the greatest and most special love any human had ever felt for any extraterrestrial being.

Everyone speculated about what the aliens thought of this. People behaved a little differently now that they felt they had an alien audience somewhere out there, but it was hard to say how exactly. They felt a kind of cosmic self-consciousness, like being narrated.

*

Llama-era Bird would have been shocked by her 2020 self, helping Dog send out voter registration forms. The bittersweet combination of love and political malaise had softened her attitude: perhaps the state could be abolished slowly and gently, or beaten into a purely redistributive form, like a sword into a plowshare, after all.

Llama-era Bird could have seen Pig coming in the violent perma-corruption of the state, but she never would have guessed that she would still be with Dog. They had met in 2013, during a time when Bird was working like crazy, in the salon and styling shoots. Dog's rent was cheap; he picked up art handler shifts now and then, wrote poetry and pined for Bird. On her rare days off, she hung out with Dog; in between fucking—giddy and playful in atmosphere, as befitted the less-interesting times—they invented new and ever more elaborate reasons why their relationship had to remain strictly casual. This was before Dog got interested in politics, before the two of them knew how to hurt each other. To Dog, Bird seemed angelic, alien: she came three times then, strangely stern amid the happiness of love, lay in bed explaining the necessity of abolishing the state.

"But what if we need it?" asked Dog.

Looking back, compared to the strange present, Bird's first few years in New York seemed freakishly chill and lacking in sudden collective accidents—but during those years she had been frustrated. She blamed President Llama for playing the false image of historical reconciliation like an instrument. He had climbed his inaugural stage to receive histrionic plaudits; "At Last" was the song that was sung. It seemed natural at the time that the first black president was figured as the entire country finally embracing a longed-for lover after centuries of loneliness. Race, Bird sometimes said she believed, was a social contraption primarily designed to make white people interested in sex.

It was the black inauguration, Bird believed, that had triggered the near-universal psychotic break that had characterized the years since. Symptomatic disaster had mounted cube-wise, at electoral intervals of four: 2008, 2012, 2016, 2020. She thrilled to the distant concept of 2024. Time had gone kind of queasy and wrong within its rigid 4/4 structure, which was known in music as common or perfect time. Irony was a dominant affect, though not the only one. Shared illusion made new things real.

Dog argued that the era of psychosis must have begun

much further back. Maybe in 2001, when 9/11 marked the impenetrable skin of world power? Bird dismissed this as too obvious. In 1971, when President Narwhal cut the regulative link between the dollar and gold and set capital free into its imaginary? In 1609, when Jamestown settlers survived the winter cannibalizing each other's flesh and dishonored a continent? In the red letter year of 1492, when Christopher Covid calculated the most astrologically auspicious moment to set sail, based on a book that predicted the end of the world in 1789?

Bird acknowledged that capital was continually shaking the world like a rag doll, but insisted that only, only, only the supreme tautology of a black president could fully break open the collective mind.

What about 1789 when a new and linear world began to end? What about the origin of agriculture and the social defeat of women? What about forty thousand years ago, when a bipedal hominid first uttered a sound that *meant* a thing, and thus meaning sprang into being to indicate and create a gap in the total mind?

No, Dog, that's too far back! Searching for an image that combined the suddenness of dramatic events with the smoothness of ongoing disaster, Bird thought of sewing, the needle puncturing the cloth over and over to form a continuous line. It was as if they all lived in anticipation of something, of teeth snapping at the thread. Still, they would rather die than admit to ever being surprised—even by aliens. Bird's friends told each other, only half joking, that black people had been in contact with aliens since prehistoric times. Dog really did feel surprised by the aliens, but maybe it was because his mom was white.

*

Several times a week, Dog came home from his call center job and made two extra hours of phone calls in his own free time for the Moley Salamanders campaign. He spoke to Christian fundamentalists, teen anarchists, elderly socialists, depressed truckers, anxious mothers, burned-out public school teachers, people who loved or hated Moley and wanted to tell him why, people who were in the middle of dinner and did not have time to talk, but did for a while anyway. He was addicted to the rush of making contact with strangers. Mostly they talked about the alien object, and Dog gently steered the conversation toward Moley's warm overtures to the aliens, his reassuring descriptions of some of the country's gentler aspirations. There was some anxiety that previous attitudes and ways of life might have been offensive or troubling to the aliens, might have cast humanity in a bad light. Americans were ready to believe that they were who Moley said they were.

The Moley campaign calls gave Dog's day a weird symmetry. In the morning and afternoon he told strangers the mostly bad news about their health insurance—that it would not refresh their opioid supply or cover their child's premature birth—and in the evening, into the night, he told different strangers the mostly good news about Moley Salamanders. Was Moley a revolutionary? No way! Universal healthcare was just good capitalist common sense. Moley was a pragmatist, sensitive to the fluctuation of possibility, not an idealist. And yet Dog's enthusiasm for Moley was so fervent that it really did shine, as Bird diagnosed, with the aura of faith. But so what if he lacked the absolute matte of grim reason? It was not that Dog spontaneously believed that a Moley presidency was possible, but that he chose to. He cried listening to Moley's speeches. He attended rallies.

"Moley Salamanders is the last hope of humanity," he and his friends told each other, though afterwards they felt a little embarrassed to have used those words, which were not current: hope, humanity.

Dog had made new friends through the Moley campaign. He knew he idealized them a little. How he saw them: experts in the weave of the social, great communicators, supportive friends. They put their friends, children and pets in their cars—they had cars and were excellent drivers—and drove the cars to different places to have healthy, engaged conversations and outdoor activities related to causes and interests before driving home emotionally intact. Their partners sat serenely in the passenger seat with a selection of nutritious snacks, right there in the car of social democracy. Dog liked how the Moley Salamanders campaign made him feel.

He was learning how to be part of something bigger than himself—not in a churchy way, he assured Bird, but in the sense that, throughout history, people had tried to put together different kinds of coalitions and ultimately had a terrible time, but the point was, the message of history was, that you had to keep trying. Why? To end urgent suffering, though admittedly at a slow, realistic pace. But it was also more than that. To repudiate once and for all the fucked-up myth that people, born from others, taught to walk and speak by others, surrounded on all sides by others and the labors of others, were self-interested and naturally individualistic. But it was also more than that.

He could see it from Bird's point of view: his political work was so absorbing that it often made him disengaged and remote. He could see why she experienced this as ironic. But it was not ironic. He could not say this to her. Of course the collective

dream was, although and because impossible to
actualize alone, a safer zone of desire and hope than
the individual dream.

*

There was a dismal sense of an almost infinitely wide,
shallow spiral of information spreading out from every
tiny event. Unable to sleep since the year turned, Dog
spent nights scrolling through news of the massive
wildfires in Australia. The burning Australian day fell
during his insomniac American night. The fire was
fluid, ongoing, intense, several and everywhere, like
the thoughts of the thousands of people he followed
online. He loved and hated to look at all this on his
personal screen.

He watched animations of how the fires spread, first
one little knuckle of fire then a finger, then a hand
and then new fingers sprouting all over, disembodied
fingers and hands of fire, then limbs and heads of
fire all over the map. It was a spreading infection or
influence. Fire colonized the fireless spaces. Warnings
flashed: *It is too late to leave. Take shelter.*

Dog tried to imagine a future time when a warning like
this would be for him. Using only a hyper-articulate
thumb, he maneuvered through traces of the
experiences of others.

In videos, settlers in the Australian wilderness wore accidental blackface of soot and ash. They wept as they explained how many hours they had been fighting the fires surrounding their property and how many generations their family had lived there. If only through the invocation of generations, they understood themselves as the children of the attempted murderers of a forty thousand year old civilization. Now they called on the remnants of that same civilization to teach them how to live with the power of destruction.

Bird murmured in her sleep.

"Sweet dreams, little alien," Dog said to her, though he did not think she could hear him.

In just three hundred years a ferocious and beautiful landscape with an ancient, careful culture braiding itself lightly into flora and fauna had been reduced to piles of charcoal and animal corpses. With these thoughts, more feelings than thoughts, churning in him, Dog watched the first light of a new day enter the room as the Guardian Australia live update reporters stopped working for the night.

"What are you doing over there?" asked Bird, newly awake. "You're so far away on your side of the bed."

"I'm just watching the fires. I was trying not to disturb you."

"Tell me about the fire," said Bird.

The fires flowing through his phone and a land he would never set foot in felt like the echo of a non-event, of the Iran war that almost happened, he told Bird. He wanted to express how deeply implicated he felt in the lives of strangers. But she had already forgotten the almost-war until he reminded her of it. Sometimes Dog was hurt when they had different feelings.

Voice hazy with recent sleep, Bird described how deeply she cared about him, compared to all those *other things*, by which she meant the news. All those other things were far away. The aliens on the beach, the assassination in Iraq, the fires in Australia, the virus in China, whatever else Dog had mentioned from one week to the next, with his head neck deep in his phone. They are out there, in everyone's world, and here we are, in our world. We can see the shared world from our world, but the shared world can't see us.

Bird was better at describing her feelings, Dog thought, so they sounded more substantial. He lost track of his sometimes, or lost interest.

His head felt heavy. He was aware of the weight of his physical head. Maybe he was getting a cold. Bird moved closer to him, reaching out a sympathetic hand to test his forehead for fever. He felt the careful weight of her hand on his head like an anchor, tethering his thoughts to his body.

FEBRUARY

The Death of Social Democracy

They had the same conversation all the time.

Bird said that nothing originated in mainstream politics, which was just a clearing house for happenstance. By pretending that an election was a revolutionary grassroots movement, the Moley Salamanders campaign would end up with neither an election victory nor a movement. If they wanted a revolution, they would have to make a revolution. Anything else was the theatrics of representation, and meanwhile a world died of itself.

Dog said that her arguments were too purist and not based on actual mass politics. They did not take into account the real behavior and beliefs of ordinary people, who did not want the radical overturning of the world. You had to begin where people were, in order to activate their sense of themselves as collective authors of their lives. That was political education.

Weren't the Christian eschatologists who heavily influenced US politics, Bird wondered, proof that the radical overturning of the world was popular?

Dog said that there was always another, more substantial reason hiding under the guise of religion. Searching for an example and not finding another, he cited European missionary zeal in Africa. They loved God as a pretext for mass murder. This was the current condition of spiritual life.

Bird said that he always underestimated belief, because of his narrow view of politics. She said that social revolution required faith in the infinite possibility that simmers underneath the movement of chance.

Then it required a god, said Dog, and therefore mass murder, given the current conditions.

A god, said Bird, is just a concept that teaches a daily life. It's like how the possibility of social transformation is kept alive by everyday practices such as crime and love of friends, practices that seem minute in comparison to the scale of the problem—race, capitalism, etc—but that reveal that the problem is unfolding in all its spectacular beauty/terror at the animal scale of a day.

She stated that an abolitionist who didn't believe in abolition in their lifetime was a reformist. The question was too urgent to be left to the glacial mechanisms of policy and politics. The anarchists knew better than the socialists what to do: smash, burn, redistribute immediately. She reminded Dog that they were living in a suicidal society in which a majority of people were surveilled, indebted, drugged and traumatized—that life itself had been dishonored.

Using information drawn from their intimate relationship, Dog suggested that she was speaking from her emotional wounds. He expressed his opinion that these wounds were not the place to generate the ethos of a mass social movement, because social movements by their nature had to move beyond the immediacy of pain and affirm that life was worth living—she herself had admitted that their terrain was everyday life. Riots did not run cities. In the end, in between admittedly welcome moments of rupture, it was all about the hard, boring work of improving local conditions, he said. Not glamorous.

Bird, too familiar with the conversation to pay attention to every detail, wondered out loud why organizers always counterposed hard, boring work to glamor. The real antithesis to being able to do hard, boring work was not a life filled with pleasure but exhaustion and/or pain. She agreed emotional wounds had no structuring capacity: though sometimes she picked her pain up thinking it could provide a strut or brick, it melted immediately in the warmth of her grasp into dark, liquid rot. And healing, with its hope of home, was not generalizable to the total social field, whose scale and variety implied a kind of homelessness. And yet the dark, liquid rot continued to stain the cloth of political aspiration: movements fell apart because of personal conflicts, because of disappointment, because everyone was so tired.

We have to keep trying, Dog said. To care for each other. To find the necessary forms of clarity and patience. To understand history. To mend what we can of what's broken. To fight our side of the class war, which we didn't choose, but is ongoing. To find ways to live. Even if it's impossible. Even more so, if it's impossible.

But why use the state, which was the law, which was the police, which was secular death, Bird wanted to know—even though she could anticipate the answer, which was just that it was there.

They wanted their differences from each other:
Dog wanted Bird to be a hopeless insurrectionist so
that he could feel his own secret fidelity to sudden
transformation still alive under layers of pragmatism
and policy; Bird wanted Dog to believe in incremental
progress in the abattoir of capitalism so that her
inner sense of abyss could acquire walls and a floor.
Bird searched in Dog for ground, and Dog searched
in Bird for the lightness of fire. Their difference
was binding and animated their love, which was
sometimes exhausting and mundane, with the five-
fingered chords of world history.

*

Despite his fervor, Dog almost didn't go to New
Hampshire to canvass for Moley Salamanders in the
Democratic primary. He was recovering from a bad
flu. His thoughts fogged easily; effort tightened his
chest. He felt newly aware of his body. His bones and
muscles felt like what they were, which was thirty
years of flesh, instead of how he wanted them to feel,
which was like himself.

Bird had gotten sick too, and they had descended
together into a weird shared dream. They were
together and apart from each other. They were sunk
in their own bodies. A seam of strangeness opened
up between them. Each at different times saw death

appear, just for a second, like a sudden glimpse of swollen red moon. The internet advised water and Advil but otherwise to just let the flu blow through them. The disease was the halo thrown off by conflicts unfolding at a cellular level. It had nothing to do with them. The body just housed this radiance and sometimes burned down.

Although Bird's fever made her strangely horny—perhaps it was the heat in the body—they did not fuck while they were sick. The shared virus took the place of sex. This proved, Bird thought, hallucinating angels in the shadows, the secret identity between sex and death. Both had the same grip around the throat.

Her fever-thoughts teemed with planetary significances. In astrology, the overlap of sex and death expressed and was expressed by the temporality of Pluto. If only she had been able to tell Dog this. Then they would not have had to be afraid of anything. Chance and fate would have been the same thing, fusing the mundane to the transcendent like a calcified ancestral bone, except that chance taught fate how to change itself. This was the source of the kaleidoscopic flickering that woke her in the night, the sign of a disturbance in the body joining forces with a disturbance in the world.

Pluto was making certain astral preparations to slot

neatly, impersonally back into where it had been when the Declaration of Independence was signed. These signatures had affirmed the new rhythm of a process incarnating death/sex as an abstract world system. They capitalized the kaleidoscope and revolutionized the institution. The power of meaning had been leached out of the world like oil. Commoditized, liquidized meaning powered fractures in the texture of relation.

Now a new Plutonic cycle was about to be born. Cosmic hour of reckoning! Shivering, Bird groped her way along the hallway to the bathroom. Her thoughts were not her own.

Carried forward by the abolition of authority and the authority of abolition, America had been born with the sun in the sign of hurt, and everyone knew what happened next. What they didn't know about was Bird's childhood.

Her psyche was organized around a scandal. Her teenage love affair with her stepbrother began during a period where her mother was—as sixteen year old Bird saw it—playing house with his father. Her mother's love-fantasy led her to impose on Bird a surreal domesticity fabricated from fragments of sitcoms and false memories. As an open attack on the family, the technically incestuous affair was Bird's greatest iconoclastic act, though apolitical because solitary and a secret.

Bird did not think that the relationship had been abusive, though she conceded privately to herself that it went on far too long. She did not think it had been abusive. She did not think so. She did not. But it had propelled her into a sense of herself as fundamentally different from, worse than, others. Or maybe she had felt like that much earlier and had reached for the transgression to anchor her sense of her innate wrongness.

Despite her conscious conviction that the whole thing was not a big deal, over the seven years of their relationship Bird had never gotten around to mentioning it to Dog. She knew that what she did not talk about revealed itself as painful through her silence. She wanted to talk about it to prove to herself that she could talk about it, that it was not painful, but she could not find a way that would not seem freighted with her previous failure to speak. All that a revelation would now communicate, via the long silence preceding it, was pain. She had decided that she did not want to be in pain. It felt stupid to be in pain; it felt stupid to have a secret. But Dog was respectful and only asked questions that he thought she wanted to answer. Perhaps she had chosen him partly because, although he was very interested in humanity in general, he was not especially curious about individuals.

Back in their sickbed, there he was, asleep and sweating with the covers thrown off. She was after all no better or worse than anyone, and had chosen him because she loved him.

On the fifth day of their illness, Bird's fever broke, and on the sixth day Dog emerged too. They showered gratefully, changed the sheets on the bed and drank black tea in their newborn kitchen. It was three days before the primary in New Hampshire. They could finally speak to each other normally again.

"I kept thinking I heard you talking in your fever," said Dog. "Something about your family."

"Moley doesn't care about black people," said Bird, deflecting.

"The great thing about universal benefits is he doesn't have to. Medicare For All would save black lives too. If that's what you're about, you should be about that."

It was not clear what Bird's position was on life and death.

"I'm going to New Hampshire," Dog said. "I know you

don't like it. But you never like it when I leave."

Bird was silent, humbled by how little she liked it.

*

A pile of recently fallen New Hampshire snow resembled something sculptural and deliberate. Dog blinked to dispel the mirage of intention and knocked at the door. It looked back at him with an unpromising surveillance eye. People wealthy enough to afford expensive tech and afraid of everyone who came to their door were not natural Moley Salamanders supporters.

Flyers left by previous canvassers were strewn around, displaying grinning faces and bullet point policies. Dog held his own stash in his hand. Every face on every flyer wore the blank, undemanding smile that passes as likable in politics and sometimes in life.

Dog was likable in that the way he looked seemed to promise something, like reconciliation with a standard or life being like a movie. He saw the woman who answered the door noting this first fact about him. She was black—in ninety-nine percent white New Hampshire! Dog relaxed, assuming an easy time.

She looked older, but he was bad at guessing. Her

beauty had a professional sheen. She was wearing an artfully shapeless gray dress with tiny pleats and an icy expression that melted a little as she looked at Dog. He felt her pleasure in looking and could take it. He asked if he could talk to her about Moley Salamanders.

"Sure, come in," the stranger said, and opened the door wide.

This happened to Dog a lot. Other canvassers had to conduct their evangelical mission from the doorstep, but Dog was often welcome inside. When he and his friends had decided to split up to cover more ground, it was tacitly understood that it made sense for Dog to knock on doors alone. Everyone looked forward to hearing later about his miracles of persuasion.

Dog's commitment to the Salamanders campaign had made him think more carefully about his effect on others. The combination of electoral political work and a lot of public discussion about identity had made him aware of himself as the bearer of signs and inheritances: young though fearful of the future, light-skinned though black, able-bodied, widely considered good-looking, a man born and raised as a man. Self description seemed like nothing at the surface—all the adjectives were so unaesthetic—but buried feelings swam up through it. For a long time, he had turned the image of how others saw him inward against himself; now, he turned it outward into politics.

"What's been on your mind lately?" he asked his mark, his eyes shining with the desire to listen.

"I don't know... What do you think about that virus in China?"

Thrown by the mention of something other than the alien object, which was all that anyone had lately wanted to talk about, Dog scrambled for an answer. "I haven't been following in detail, but it seems like they have it under control. If you're interested in health issues—have you heard of Moley Salamanders?"

"You must realize I watch the news."

"I bet you've heard some interesting things about him on TV."

"They say he's a communist. That's a communist? It makes me laugh. Of course, China is supposed to be communist too, and they're in a mess."

"All the other rich countries have some form of universal healthcare," said Dog, conscious of the obligation to make his voice sound warm and sincere. The ersatz of familiarity draped over a conversation between strangers was basically sales patter, no matter how good the intention. It was weird that she had said the word *communist* a bunch of times. "Americans don't like things that have to be given to everyone," said the stranger. "We want to be exceptional."

"People change their minds once they have what they need," countered Dog. "Universal healthcare isn't controversial anywhere it's been introduced. It unites all sides of politics. People want to be healthy, they want to live."

"It's good to be optimistic. It's not for me, but it's good. Maybe if the plague takes a lot of us, people will change their minds."

Unsure how to respond, Dog reverted to boilerplate Moley boosterism.

"This is the first political campaign I've worked on," he said. "There are things that I disagree with Senator Salamanders on, but one thing is important to me: that people living in the United States should be able to get whatever medical attention they need without having to worry about debt or destitution."

"That won't happen," she said. "I'm not saying it's a bad idea. I'm just saying it won't happen. You're young, so you can still dream."

"Moley is seventy and still working to make his dreams real."

"You're right, time has nothing to do with it."

She smiled at him with an actor's professional intimacy, as if she, too, wanted to seem other than how she felt.

It often occurred to Dog, phoning strangers or knocking on their doors, puncturing the plena of strangers' lives, that people were not in the habit of thinking of their needs as bare facts, like a plant's need for water and light. Every basic social service had to be pitched as if it were an innovation, despite that people could not live without the mutual provision of shelter, food and medicine. Life had to be constantly argued for and financially evaluated, and this process thinned out reality and made it feel airy and contingent.

On the other hand, in some ways the more atomized perspective came closer to the truth. People made to perform as individualized competitors in a market were not wrong to feel isolated from each other. The state was a complicated source of care, because it mainly entered into everyday life to demand or threaten.

Dog imagined that Moley would be impatient with this kind of thinking. It was not practical. Practicality was a hallmark of his campaign, both rhetorically and politically. Canvassers were advised not to argue too hard with the people they met. They were advised to look for points of agreement and if they could not find any, they were advised to leave.

"I agree with you that this country has deep problems," Dog said, carefully, because he did not want to leave. "And the presidency is not a radical institution—maybe there's no such thing as a radical institution. But this campaign is about a whole movement, not just an individual politician."

She seemed unmoved by the movement. He had the sudden, strange feeling that he was continuing a conversation with Bird, that the stranger was another incarnation of Bird. Dog wondered for the first time if the aliens would be able to do anything for humanity.

"If it brings you joy, I will go out there and put in my vote for Moley," said the stranger who was not Bird, as Bird had also promised. "But it won't make any difference."

"A vote is a vote, but it would bring me joy if you would believe for once that things could be different."

"Well, then we will have to find some other way."

It was not unusual for lonely people to flirt with Dog, but it was unusual for him to feel so reluctant to cut the conversation short and leave. He knew that bitches were crazy, i.e. possessed by divine reason, and he deeply sympathized—however, this meant it was important to preserve a certain level of autonomy from women. Yet his eyes followed without question when the stranger gestured toward the TV. On the mute screen, a lizard-like creature sifted through a pile of jewels.

"They're showing everything they can think of about aliens," she said. "It's all anyone wants to watch. It's bringing all kinds of things to the surface. Shows no one has seen for years. I was in this show when I was twenty-five years old. I had only just moved to Los Angeles. I was very beautiful then. I lived in my car for six weeks, then I landed the job. 1992. It was more money than I ever had before in my life. I bought a fur coat. White mink. The weather was all wrong for it. I don't know what I was thinking. Fur was my central image of luxury. Luxury had something to do with suffering, but not mine or not this time. I turned the AC up high and I walked around in my two thousand dollar fur."

"I don't know the show," Dog admitted.

"No one does. It tanked completely. It's called *Fossa and the Ancient Aliens*. My name is Fossa."

"You played the lead?"

"No, just a coincidence. Fossa is my real name. I had a supporting role. Could have developed into more, but there was only one season in the end. It wasn't a bad show. I was surprised to see it again. Now I can't watch anything else."

"So you predicted the aliens," Dog said. "Pretty impressive."

"Yes," said Fossa, sincerely.

Onscreen, the lizard had selected a stone and was carving something on it, an alphabet. He was showing a group of humans how to shape the letters. They were watching avidly. Their eyes shone with attraction to knowledge. The alien warned them to beware of the abstractions that written language would inevitably introduce. They did not seem to listen.

"I bought a new car," said Fossa. Where were they? They were in Nashua, 2020, and Los Angeles, 1992. "A Lexus. I had to make monthly payments. Give me your favorite new car, I said to the salesman. He could have sold me anything. I would have paid a million dollars. I thought I was about to be a movie star. But he took pity on me and sold me a car I could just about afford. I paid monthly. I thought I was all that in my Lexus. But it was only a car—not freedom, just a car. Do you drive?"

Dog said yes, but he didn't own a car.

"You should get a car. It helps you get reconciled to the concept of sudden death. Some kids keyed my car during the riots. Little black kids. There was a general sense of abandon. I got out of the car and I yelled at them. That stopped them in their tracks, seeing a black woman get out of that car. I yelled at them so loud. Don't fuck with my fucking car. And then I cried. Right there in the parking lot. It was downtown. They all looked at me. I was so beautiful then, but I couldn't stop crying. You could smell the smoke from a fire somewhere. Everybody wants to feel free. It was only a car, but the way I acted you would have thought it was physically part of me. I thought my heart would break. But it didn't."

"I'm glad," said Dog.

"You're a sweet boy. Pass me that ashtray. Do you want to hear a story about the president?"

Fossa's story was that long ago she had a friend who briefly dated the president. He wasn't the president then. The friend didn't think much of him, but she got by financially on the admiration of men, so she tolerated his company. Back then, he was just as much of an asshole, but he had a wider range of human affects. It was before his personality had contracted into a single, desperate note.

One night the future president took Fossa's friend to Corona Park. He said he wanted to tell her a secret. She didn't care. That was her role in life: men told her things, and she didn't care. She was like a silent priest in a confession booth, but more beautiful and tangible. The future prez was sentimental about the park, where the World's Fairs of 1938 and 1965 had taken place. He told Fossa's friend all about it. Despite Fossa's friend's duty as a semi-professional beauty to be bored by rich men, one detail had bothered her so much that she ended up repeating it to Fossa.

Fossa continued to watch TV as she told the story, and Dog watched Fossa. Who watched Dog? Aliens, maybe.

A time capsule had been buried in the earth to mark the World's Fair, intended to be opened after five thousand years had passed. The president had hired an archaeologist to locate it. He had it dug up and opened it. He had done this, he told Fossa's friend, because he did not believe that there would be five thousand years of future. This is it, he said. The end of the line. This is the future.

"Isn't that how it feels?" asked Fossa, concluding her story.

"Not to me," said Dog.

"Stay a while," said Fossa, smiling, smiling.

"I have a girlfriend."

Fossa laughed for a long time. Mouth open as if he meant to say something else, Dog watched her laugh. After she stopped laughing and he closed his mouth, they had sex.

*

As Dog drove back to the campaign office to drop off his clipboard and leftover flyers, he mentally prepared a story adjacent to reality about a crazy old lady who had kept him talking for too long. He had what felt at a glance like hundreds of text messages and missed calls from his friends, none of which he felt ready to deal with. It was around 10pm.

Outside the office, there was a girl crying. She had severe gothic bangs, home-applied black nail polish and a long-sleeve Moley 2020 tee under her purple North Face. Dog wondered who had made her cry. When he asked if she was okay, she cried harder.

"Are you here with friends?" he asked.

"They got in an accident," she sobbed.

"Your friends?" An alternate timeline briefly presented itself in the moment before he understood what she was about to say.

"Your friends," she said.

Dog's grandmother had died the year before, and Dog had sat with her as she entered deeper and deeper into the country of her death. It was as if a first official day of dying had been declared, and after that there was a smooth descent with no holding place. Looking back, the time he had spent with her then seemed highly saturated. That was how the days of dying were: color and sensation were more deeply invested in them. He had a vivid sense-memory of the paper-smooth texture of her culminated palm. She had died angry and sad. She said she saw the way the world was going (mass death, destruction, ugliness). Dog said he saw how it had always been (mass death, destruction, ugliness). In retrospect the difference seemed hardly important—the dead disparaged sequence. But Dog and his grandmother had argued more and more towards the end of her life, before she became too sick and tired to have opinions. Dog tried to believe their disagreements had been a sign of how much they loved each other. The special horror of her death had been its absolute ordinariness. But his friends' deaths were not like that. When his grandma died, time folded back in on itself and pressed down, printing, insisting—now, it splintered.

This is the craziest year of my life, he thought, already.

Dog went into the office and they gave him the news. The friends he had travelled up with had gotten into an accident on the I-93. The tires lost their grip on black ice and in the darkness they slid into the opposite lane, where a truck slammed into their car. Two had died—"passed away," the kind Moley volunteers said—at the scene of the accident, and one was in the ICU. Their families had been notified and were on their way. The concerned volunteers offered Dog food, tea, alcohol, their homes.

"It's okay. I'm staying with a friend," Dog said. "I think it's best if I just go and be with my friend."

"You must be in shock," they all said sympathetically. He felt nothing, but perhaps that was what they meant.

He drove back to Fossa's place. She was still awake, watching the news. She didn't seem surprised to see him.

"The virus turned up in Seattle," she said. "Why are you crying?"

"In my heart of hearts, I know Moley can't win," said Dog.

MARCH

The Brotherhood of Man

Bird waited in the apartment she shared with Dog. Was waiting her destiny, her gender?

All through the end of February and the first days of March, the news became more and more like dense cloud. The alien object, kept in a high-security military facility upstate while the government ran tests, grew legs and walked out on the first day of the month.

A panicked search began. The alien object seemed to be able to make itself invisible, or to cover incredible distances fast. In any case it could not be found. Eye witnesses who had seen the object break out of its scientific jail described the oak-like surface peeling back to reveal something that looked like dark-red skin. Eight limbs sprouted from its sides. It walked out spider-like, blinking three enormous, red-lidded eyes. *Don't be sad*, one shocked Marine could swear it said as it left. Then it was gone. There was speculation that it had given up on Earth—that Earth had failed a test.

Dog had called and said he had to stay in New Hampshire, for some reason, a car accident, an investigation? There had been a death or several. The conversation was cloudy too. *Come back*, is not what Bird said. She was under the power of a secret censor. So when Dog stopped replying to her texts and calls, she was helpless to tell him or herself anything. It was as if the part of him that could speak to her had died in the accident.

Thinking about when she last saw him, declaring his social-democratic intentions as they sat in survival sunlight at the kitchen table, Bird wondered if the fever had dislodged something in his soul. She saw a leviathan tail from her fever dreams slapping against the total surface of the Atlantic like a fumbled dive, conjuring tsunamis and earthquakes, setting forth a disturbance that reached from the shoreline through the city to their block. Already it had swept Dog away. Vibrating with premonition in her empty bed, she felt a hard future coming.

In the first week of Dog's absence, Bird stopped eating. In the second week, she stopped sleeping. Then, running out of major functions to slash from her life, she called her stepbrother in London. It was a sudden decision, and she regretted it even as she made the call. But she pushed through the feeling of discomfort until she heard his soft, definite, familiar voice. His name was Alpaca. He told Bird to come home.

"London is not my home," said Bird.

"And New York is?"

Home was not a word that Bird took personally. But, at a loss for what to do with what felt like a newly vacant life, she booked a flight to London. It was March 5th. Winter had never really gotten hold of the year, but now its grip was so loose that bright, spacious days began to fall from it. She cleared the fridge of everything capable of rot and scrubbed the kitchen cupboards inside and out. She was sustained by manic energy, empty of calories or rest. She left a note on Dog's desk, the basic axiom of her heart: FUCK YOU I LOVE YOU FOREVER.

She got a taxi to JFK. Her plane took off smoothly. It was March 9th. In retrospect the dates would seem like monuments to her mistake. She ate a meal in tiny plastic compartments, watched an episode of a TV show about aliens, then took two Xanax and slept for five hours. When she woke up, the patchwork fields of evil England were visible below. Each line represented, she thought, filtering original accumulation through a Xanax haze, a deep cut in the social. Wounds, wounds. Had Dog been right all along that a wound could generate nothing? What was the source of his belief, then, in the global proletariat that had bled out from these million torturous cuts?

Alpaca picked her up at Heathrow. London looked gray. The light was thin, so unlike the cushiony light of New York City. There was construction everywhere. It was a city permanently in construction. It was like someone always claiming to be on the verge of a personal revelation. In this way it was a little like Alpaca, who had been doing a lot of meditation, he said, really a lot. She had forgotten how relentlessly he clung to the idea of epiphany.

He told Bird he was making big changes in his life. He was applying for jobs elsewhere, in Dakar, in Shanghai. She expressed surprise.

"It wouldn't be till next year," he said. "Europe is over. Can you feel it? The whole continent is over. It's over. America is over too. France is over, Italy is over, England is the most over of all."

"What's happening with the virus? With the aliens? I haven't looked at the news for a few days."

"I don't read the news," said Alpaca, "it stresses me out."

"Not even about the aliens?"

Alpaca's face was smooth and scornful. "That whole thing is a hoax."

She hated it when she saw a way in which they were the same. But it was also a relief from the loneliness of her sense of obscene singularity. This was the dangerous frequency of feeling between them.

"It came alive and escaped," she said. "On the first. I remember the date because I remember thinking, 'At least now I know Dog won't come back in February.'"

"People say all sorts of things," said Alpaca, confidently. "They swear they've seen impossible things with their own eyes. I don't fall for it. I'm aware. I have my eyes open. I'm not walking around just believing things like that."

Alpaca did not need to consume any news because, he said, he found inspiration and meaning in the details of his immediate surroundings: ads for financial services, late night trips to the supermarket, shelled pistachios, the haunted face of a stranger—anything, really, anything.

He talked like this for a long time, as they sat in traffic on the M4. The landscape was unfamiliar in its grim familiarity. Bird thought that, like everyone else, Alpaca did not know where his desire came from. Even though everyday life was so replete with...*things*... didn't he want to follow the news to understand what was happening in politics? No, because he did not believe in politics. He believed that everything was theater. He believed protest or struggle of any kind was theater. He hated his father, Bird's stepfather, and worshipped his mother, who Bird had never met: that was not theater. Although he had inherited his father's strong nose and skill with machines, he had always wanted to be more like his mother, who had been a free spirit, he said. So free he hadn't seen her in twenty years, Bird knew, but she said nothing. She felt a sense of smallness like looking at stars when she thought about all the ways people were hurt by experiences they were afraid to understand. Alpaca was still talking—nervously, she realized. He was pointing out municipal improvements since her last visit.

"Must be boring compared to New York," he said.

She hated how Alpaca said *New York*: both awed and contemptuous, because he thought that living there meant she thought she was better than him. But he was the reason she did not feel able to live in London. She did not know why she had come back. She felt the first stirrings of awareness of the extent of her mistake.

They pulled up outside an unfamiliar house.

"I got you an Airbnb," said Alpaca.

"Oh," said Bird. "I thought I was staying with you."

"I don't feel like that would be...it seems like...you know how things are."

Bird said she didn't understand, but she didn't want to argue. This was in itself argument, but Alpaca did not reply. His silence, although momentary, felt deep and final. At last he asked if she wanted help with her bags. She got out of the car. They had a brief struggle over her luggage, ending with Bird's insistence that she could carry it into the house herself.

He helped her find the key, and together they entered an absolutely featureless apartment. It looked like it had been designed according to a principle of total equality to make exactly no one feel at home. I could die here, Bird thought to herself, but it didn't mean anything: it was a reflex thought, like the twitch of an overworked muscle. Give or take local conditions, anyone could live or die anywhere. Those were the rules—or else why had Bird always moved around so easily, as if there was no reason for her to be anywhere?

"Would you like to come for dinner tomorrow night?" asked Alpaca, not meaning it.

"No thank you," said Bird, obedient to the unspoken but more urgent demand.

She sat down on the gray couch and covered her face with her hands. Planetary exhaustion suffused her, not jet lag, not even human.

Alpaca hovered, unable to leave. They both had tension in their chests in the shape of the unspeakable. It was as if their silence were speaking it. By saying even one direct word they could stop this silent speech, and this was all that either of them wanted to do. But they could not say anything directly.

"I'm so stupid," she said, in despair.

"You're not stupid," he said.

He was as far away as Dog, but further, because he had never been close. Dog was real and had been kind to her, and Alpaca was the abyss.

"When people say they're stupid, they mean stupid about themselves," said Bird.

"I wish I could support you, but I have to think of my

kids," said Alpaca.

That shut her up.

Alpaca left and Bird went to bed for three days, waking only to dose herself with more Xanax or force herself to eat. On the third day, she woke up in the afternoon into the realization that she could not stay in England and live. She booked a flight online. She texted her brother that she was leaving. *Sorry we didn't get to spend time*, he wrote back. The unspeakable pulsed, once, hard, in her chest, and then she shut it away again, in her liver or kidney or wherever it lived when she could not feel it.

On the appointed day, she packed her bags and went to the airport. It was crazy there. When she asked at the information desk what was going on, they told her that President Pig had closed the borders and she would not be permitted to return home. The catastrophe was personal/impersonal, like the Leo/Aquarius polarity in astrology. Her mind reached for this comforting abstraction amid concrete tumult. The coronavirus had migrated from the news directly into her life.

*

Coronatime: the crown of time had closed around everyone.

Restaurants, public buildings and malls were still open, and the streets were still full of people. Surreal to walk like a ghost or a prophet around a world you believed to be about to end. Bird moved around the neighborhood in a trance, trying to keep her distance from others. She had started wearing masks since her attempt to fly home had abruptly brought her in line with plague reality. Medical supply chains were overwhelmed but she found handmade cotton masks online, decorated with inappropriately non-apocalyptic flowers—Etsy had sprung into action faster than the government. But hardly anyone in London was on her fear level. Her mask triggered a weird, wondering look in strangers, the look of a repressed fear getting dislodged. It didn't matter: all this activity would stop soon. The streets would be empty. Some of these strangers, along with their strange gazes, would be dead.

There were these little sci-fi lurches. When she could not believe it was real. She told herself: you will feel better when you accept it. And eventually she did. The lurching feeling of reality reorienting into nightmare went away. Instead a dull buzzing took up space in her head.

The virus was reshaping the world. Perhaps this was the real alien invasion. Where were the aliens? They had gone silent. A global feeling of rejection descended on the Earth.

Forget the aliens. (Easy enough for Bird.) Where were the pandemic interventions? After assuring everyone that the virus could be contained if everyone washed their hands more carefully, the government admitted that millions could die. Bird's hands were very dry. The government declared dramatic measures, too late. She anointed her dry hands with shea butter and olive oil and then put on disposable gloves. It was not clear if gloves helped slow the transmission of the virus, though they provided a convenient deep moisturizing opportunity. It was clear, in that moment, that governance existed to repress life, rather than secure it.

Let everyone else lose their minds as the crown of time tightened; Bird was already grimly reconciled. Alone under national lockdown, in an apartment drastically lacking in detail, she went down into a void as familiar as a childhood home.

In the void she was surprised to find walls and a floor, even furniture, chairs and a table picked out by someone else
In the void she saw her grandmother curled over her sewing in failing light void light, when Bird went to switch on the lamp above the grandmother's blank gaze stopped her in her tracks what's that okay no strong light in the void

She saw Alpaca at sixteen turning to her with his hair
grown out a little too long, blurred lines and edges
In the void she saw all her good and bad decisions, she
revisited her decisions, but could she call them that,
blown through her life by wild intensity of feeling? She
picked up each pseudo-decision and weighed it in her
hand, sitting on a dark chair at a dark table, her mind
and body covered over with darkness
In the void she tried saying her name out loud now
and then to remind herself her being had tangible
contours from without if not from within, she thought
about what the name meant to others, what it meant
to her, kind of arbitrary and specific both at the same
time, just a name, kind of slung onto her body at
birth that she had kept, she had held onto, because
she wanted to have been named by her parents or
she did not really think about it until now, Bird, Bird,
perhaps her mother had looked up from the childbirth
bed where her life was decisively ruined by Bird's
hapless passage into it and seen a shape circling
too far up in the sky—a hawk, a falcon?—no, too far
up to be anything more than an idea of a bird, Bird,
events happen without necessary detail and pass
immediately out of view
Mothers birds skies distances visions mothers
Could she fully become a person if unreflected in
the first eyes that saw her or was she doomed to live
with parts missing like a medical miracle with only
a blasted fragment of liver, a torn shred of spleen, a

boneless wing on which childhood had left signs of
greed or hunger, teethmarks
Want and need cannot after all be cleanly
distinguished so that even someone as dedicated to
feeling as Bird could walk too far in the direction of an
outside authority that she knew on some level it was
her destiny to abolish in herself
In the void she understood that the very thin threads
that had held her mind in the space of sanity all her
life were relationships with others but in the void she
could not find these, she could only find images and
memories, mothers and false brothers
She thought of Dog, in the void Dog was the pain of
loss and inside the pain of loss was the void, she could
still stand in line for the supermarket still sometimes
stumble through the motions of morning coffee
evening food though sometimes she forgot, at those
times she realized by her flagging sense of reality that
she had not eaten, as if and perhaps really resurfacing
from a trance to find that it was Tuesday or September
or the end
She smoked a pack of cigarettes a day, once a week
she had to go outside to get them, thank you god for
her addiction to tobacco a sacred plant thank you
Big Tobacco that alone propelled her out of the house
and into the glancing contact with others by which
she remembered her responsibility to not be a fucking
idiot and die, in fact you could tell she wanted to live
by how many cigarettes she smoked, her addiction

preserved her desire to live like an insect in amber i.e. not actively but ready to be reanimated, life clothed in death is the form of a seed, seven packs a mask and no eye contact, thank you I don't need a bag

Mice entered the void, ants, dust

The presence of others was as overwhelming as their absence, the presence of strangers in the street, the exterminator who entered the void with giant hands and a toolkit saying don't worry they die easily it's like the flu they just lay down and die

Dear Dog, she said in her head, hi Dog it's been a while I'm thinking of you I hope you are well, I am not well, I hope it doesn't seem like I'm tugging on your sympathies, hope it doesn't seem in any way like like my clammy hand is gripping the sleeve of your sympathies, now that everyone has retreated into their private difficulty or ease

She hated the weather no matter how good or bad it was

She thought of their friends, Dog's dead friends Turtle and Wolf, her living friends Heron, Dolphin, Leopard, who did not call her, and she did not call them, now in the time of the void the void entered in between them and it peeled them away from each other until there was only Bird a threadless thread

Was it possible this was the final decree the final say that the void was the final judgment on her life, which she had wanted to do violence to, why was that, to forgive her mother, to attract her attention, to undo the accident of Alpaca, it was too long ago to reconstruct, easier to let the parts fray and become formless, she moved through the void as if she was herself a tiny void, the void's impossible daughter sent far away from home when discovered at evil play one day screaming commotion fury but what was the real source of their anger and disgust, it could not be the simple fact of the boy turning to her smiling in repulsive memory

What could you do you only had a body and the body could only do a few things it had a few tricks it was strange to sit motionless on her void bed with her unseen body in monochromatic dawn and try to remember the actual sensations of fucking

In the void she believed that although she would one day leave the void some part of it would never leave her, she called Alpaca, he did not pick up, if Alpaca had picked up what Bird would have said is I should have wrapped my mind in something going into this, I should have taken something close to hand like Dog or a child or a job and wrapped it around my mind so my mind would not be naked to experience whatever this is that the void is only a name for

*

She had to get home. It seemed impossible.

A week or two into her total solitude, Alpaca turned up at her door. He was altered by the new circumstances, but in the opposite direction from Bird. He seemed energized, inspired. He had started a volunteer-run food delivery service for black elders in the community, he said. He used the word *community* a lot now.

"Who will look after our own if we won't?" he asked, at top volume, as Bird made tea and searched for mugs in a pile of dirty dishes.

She stared at him blankly. She was re-acclimating to the sight of another person. "Who will what?"

"Look after our own. Black elders. Bird, don't you care about anything?"

"I guess not."

"I'm here to ask for your help. I'm here to call you to your best self. Mutual aid is the best of our community, pulling together in a crisis."

"You sound like the government."

"You've become cynical, Bird."

"*Cynical is the least of what I've become*," she hissed, and he stepped back from her instinctively, then made an exaggerated expression of concern. She could see him consciously assemble it.

"Baby bird," he said, in a long-ago tone. "Big Bird. What's going on? What's gotten into you? Now, I know this hasn't been an easy time..."

She had a hard lump in her throat. Like every affliction then, it felt like it would be with her forever. It would go on, like March 2020, for one thousand years. Her body would disintegrate around it, leaving only the diamond in her throat, and when that was over there would be nothing left.

"I'm sorry. You're right, it's been a hard time. I'd be happy to help."

They drove out to Croydon. She felt nothing for the familiar landscape. They parked outside an apartment building. Alpaca offered her a hazmat suit from the trunk of the car.

"Where did you get these? Isn't there a shortage?"

"God provides."

She felt huge and airy in it, like Mousey Elephant billowing with her own words in the video for "The Rain". The image was incongruous in the bleak circumstance and made her laugh. Alpaca looked at her with suspicion, perhaps fear, then once again smoothed his gaze out into neutrality. She felt herded and managed like a cow. He handed her an N95 mask with a filter, the kind that was lately almost impossible to get.

"You're busy on the black market."

"Mind your language."

"The informal market. Isn't it safer to just leave the food outside the door?"

"No, you have to spend time with them. It's for their mental health, you know."

"Tell me about this one, then," Bird suggested.

"Horse. He's about eighty years old. He was in prison for a long time so he doesn't have a lot of people coming round. He has dementia—gets stuck in different parts of his life. That's what it's like for most of them, to be honest, when they get to a certain age. I'm not looking forward to the past."

"Alpaca, don't you think it's really stupid?"

"Nah, aging is normal, it's God's will."

"I mean don't you think it was stupid, how things were, when we were kids."

"I don't know why you always want to talk about that."

"I never say anything!"

Alpaca got out of the car. "Come on then."

The inside of Horse's building smelled of damp and urine. The elevator was broken and the red-painted stairs took sharp, elaborate turns. As Bird followed obediently behind Alpaca, a macabre, involuntary daydream about being taken to the gallows autoplayed in her mind. These were her last steps. The red floor was her last landscape. What century was it? Contemporary sirens in the distance intruded. It was always just 2020. It would probably, Bird thought with sudden panic, be 2020 forever. Like how parts of the 1960s had yet to end.

Horse's place looked unchanged since sometime in the 1990s. Alpaca took sure, familiar footsteps through the small living room and into the bedroom, as Bird meekly followed behind. There were political and spiritual posters on the wall that she recognized from a childhood spent mired in adult obsessions—not unusefully, though the atmosphere of conspiracy, she often thought, had been bad for her developing sense of reality. She had never got the hang of self-evident fact, though she had learned to simulate belief in it, her learned glibness concealing her sense of a tightly woven world.

There was black Jesus with his right hand held up serenely, a golden halo around the black halo of his hair, wearing a blue cloak. The historically implausible availability of blue dye had not been corrected alongside Christ's melanism, because objects could not suffer. There was a red, black and green Africa silhouette in slatted wood. This was Bird's only memorable cartographical instruction, the only continent she could draw from memory—though she had never been there, partly because she felt embarrassed by the more baroque manifestations of the concept of home.

There was Malcolm X in what she now knew was his final, craziest year. There was not one light-brown black man capable of fury who did not in some way remind her of her father. Or perhaps, knowing him only as much as he would allow, she had taken the average of a room of images like this and fused them with her experiences to make a composite father. The living room decor was a father to her, or part of one.

"Mind if I leave you here with him for a bit?" asked Alpaca.

"With who?"

"Horse! Bird, what's wrong with you today?"

"I've been alone a lot recently. All the time, in fact."

Alpaca's father was more the silent type. She did not remember much about him, though from five years sharing a home with him and living as a strange, unhappy family she had the impression of a weak striving for goodness, easily obliterated by the power of his wife/her mother's desire to suffer. She had no opinion of him. If someone told her he had died, she would say, *Sorry for your loss.*

Alpaca got ready to leave. "I'll be back in an hour, okay?"

She looked at Horse, on the bed. She wanted him to look like her father, but Horse was thinner and darker and dying.

"We have to come from somewhere," she said. "Even if it's outer space."

"Call this food?" asked Horse.

They listened to Alpaca leave. His heavy footsteps receded. A door slammed shut behind him, then another. Then the thick atmosphere of world closed around him, erasing the sound of his movements. Bird had a brief, habitual daydream in which he never came back. Her thoughts that day were iced with unwanted fantasy. As if to affirm the vision, a car screeched away outside.

Bird and Horse sat in silence for a while.

"How has your day been?" she tried.

"Call this food?" he asked again.

She understood he was elsewhere, though here with her.

"Alpaca didn't introduce us," she said. "I'm Bird."

"I'm here the same reason anyone is. Because I've been unlucky," said Horse.

Yes, by his half-seeing eyes, she understood that he was sunk more deeply in the past than Alpaca had described. The lump in her throat relaxed.

"We were in that stupid little house, pretending to be something no one wanted, which was a family," she said. "What do you think about that?"

"They wouldn't treat animals like this. They do animals worse in the end. Though you don't know how they feel about it compared to us."

"I used to think you get older and the past falls away. But it comes closer. I think about it all the time. It's a kind of emblem or a shield. It used to stand in between me and Dog. Like I was hoarding secret proof that he couldn't love me. I think that's how it was."

"I think animals do know. It's us who don't know. The question is how to get the government out of the head." His accent was reassuringly Jamaican despite the odd content of his speech.

"It's really stupid that we had sex," she said. "That's the main thing I think about, when I think about it. I feel embarrassed—ashamed of having been born, is that possible? But why is shame my only feeling for my life?"

Horse's eyes rolled deeply back in his skull and then appeared to be swallowed by his forehead, to return as three new eyes, round and black. The dark skin of Horse's body glowed a dull red. The multiple lids of his three eyes fluttered. His skin slowly took on a new texture and color, something like polished oak.

Bird immediately accepted that an alien had inhabited Horse's body. In the moment, this did not seem strange to her, any more or less than his dementia.

"I have to express my gratitude," said the alien, in a creaky whisper, as if getting used to having a voice. "We are activated by signs of basic culture, such as the incest taboo."

"Where are you from?"

"We are working on how to communicate our concept of place to you."

Bird didn't know what to say to that. The alien was silent for a while too.

"What are these memories?" he said. "I feel them inside this body. Very disturbing."

"Prison," said Bird.

"*Prison*."

"It means the government has the power to lock someone up, to prevent them from leaving, make them not free. It's complicated. There are biology fetishists running the money machines. I don't know how much time you have."

"Like what they did to me."

"Basically, yeah."

Bird looked at Horse and the alien, together in one body. She wondered what she would forget when she was old. Even this? Of course the aliens, like every expansionist people in the world no matter how extraordinary and benign, had to arrive by appropriating the body of a black person. She missed Dog acutely. Their love had been a kind of safety.

"Are you afraid of me?" asked the alien, after a while.

"I don't feel my feelings as they're happening. I feel them a little while afterwards."

"Biologically?"

"I don't know."

"You're an interesting species. Some of us think you have potential, and some of us think you're a mess."

"It's a combination of both of those, pretty much, I think."

"Should we stay or go, in your opinion?"

"Stay. Why not? It's a strange time. Maybe something good will come of it. I'm sorry, I'm very depressed."

"I'm thinking of going south," said Horse's body. "Do you think I will find anything different there? Anything not prison?"

"Probably not, to be honest," said Bird.

"Should I go back to America?" asked Horse.

"Don't start there. Start somewhere else. Go to Cuba. Go to Iran."

"Iran?"

"No, sorry, that was stupid, don't go to Iran. Go to Cuba."

"*Cuba.*"

"Tell them they won. Tell them they did the best. They tried to look after people. They won the alien ethics test."

"Okay," said Horse's mouth, lungs, larynx etc.

APRIL

First Season

In the pilot episode of *Fossa and the Ancient Aliens* a paradigmatically ordinary white girl living in the suburbs, named Fossa, falls into a well. Market analysis suggested the public were interested in supernatural stories in which a beautiful white girl kicked ass—the show was a creative endeavor born from aggregated calculation more than inspiration or any other kind of individuated quest for meaning. So in some ways, you could argue, it concentrated the texture of its time more intensely than the autonomous artwork. At the same time, the show's impersonality provided, for those viewers who became inexplicably attached to it during the first pandemic spring, a kind of safety or retreat from feeling, at a time when sensitivities of all kinds had become freighted with the actuality of mass death and sickness.

Fossa watched for different reasons: to see herself almost thirty years previously, to relive her life, to absorb herself in the strange semi-reality of the passage of time.

She was still beguiled by the coincidence between her name and the name of the main character, even though she had played a different role. It pleased her because it proved that, like the erratic movements of a stock market, reality was recursive and absolutely contingent.

Dog did whatever Fossa felt like doing. Lately he had no will of his own.

> The suburb Fossa lives in is quiet. Upheaval passes through as disturbing headlines in the evening broadcast, leading to bad dreams; in the mornings the men shake off these dreams by taking care of their car or lawn; women the same with kitchen and hair. Everyone produces commodities and services of value to their community. Homes are free of contamination and when the police arrive, it is by trusting invitation and in welcome. The suburb is majority white, with one black family, who act white, and one Peruvian family, who act Mexican. In this world even the intimate shocks of sex and love are adorably

trivial. Solitude is banned, but only because it lacks the kinetic energy of narrative, which must be magnetized by the inevitability of marriage. That's how the forward propulsion of history gets up off the mortality floor, according to TV.

Dog and real-life Fossa had seen the show so often that they could follow the plot even while barely paying attention. Fossa told Dog that the film director Krzysztof Kieslowski stopped making documentaries and turned to fiction movies because he wanted to show someone crying alone in their room, a logical impossibility in a documentary. She mentioned this while scrolling on her phone. She observed that now you could watch anyone crying alone in their room, and it felt like both documentary and fiction. This part of the episode bored her a little because her character, Iguana, had yet to appear.

Dog felt suddenly claustrophobic in Fossa's house. Real-life Fossa's fascination with her own onscreen image had at first charmed him, then disturbed him, and now he felt nothing about it. Time had got either very compressed or very stretchy, he wasn't sure which—in any case, if someone had told him he had been at Fossa's for a year, he would have had no trouble believing it. He had been wearing the same clothes for weeks, having added to his three-day canvassing wardrobe only an oversize terrycloth bathrobe of Fossa's that he wore around the house. Leaving real Fossa in the steady glow of the TV and fictional Fossa inside it, he went to Target to buy new underwear.

What draws the fictional Fossa toward the well and its promise of falling? It could be fate, speaking to her from the ground, or a secret desire to harm herself, or simple curiosity, like a reader feels when opening a book. Her fall is sudden–darkness fills the screen. When she wakes up, back on the ground, she has no memory of what has happened. Her clothes and skin are covered in thick, lightly sparkling dust.

A local amateur archeologist is excited by the discovery of the well. Through rudimentary tests, he establishes that the well is, astonishingly, several thousand years old! How old exactly is hard to say–he needs a lab. He visits Fossa in the hospital to tell her his preliminary findings. The amateur scientist, Bobcat, is tall, handsome, shy, dorky, with a great body. Fossa is a beautiful college freshman with golden hair and a fun sense of humor. Her Aryan good looks and bubbly nature belie her penetrating intelligence. An as-yet-fragile air bubble of romantic future forms and surrounds the two of them. But when Bobcat tells Fossa that the well seems to be ancient, she instantly has a seizure. Nurses rush to her side. Bobcat leaves. On his way, he takes an item of her clothing, still covered in dust from her fall. It's a shirt or something–not completely free of sexual significance, but not too weird.

The events of the show, so far mundane, are lent intensity and depth by the subtle magic of the edit and by the beauty of the actors.

Dog waited in line outside Target. Everyone seemed tense, especially the unmasked people making light of the pandemic out loud as they waited to enter under the big red and white eye. Their voices were clipped at the edges like unmixed sound. Nothing flowed anymore between people. There was only viral transmission. The pandemic was gaining an ugly social shape, both baggy and clinging, wool and water. The year was falling further in.

He wandered the store mindlessly for half an hour without being able to find anything he needed. It felt like too huge an effort to ask a worker where the socks were. He realized that he had not seen or spoken to anyone apart from Fossa and TV in five weeks. He wandered around Target crying, crying. It was as if a whole world had been lost. A view of the past opened up, giving dimension to the flat expanse of his present. He saw Bird very vividly in his mind. The future ached as emptiness, while brands shimmered as pre-plague hieroglyphs: he threw plastic-wrapped packages of Hanes socks and Fruit of the Loom boxer briefs, the consumer choices he had made long ago by natal right, into his big red Target cart. Masked shoppers scrubbed their hands with sanitizer and walked the one-way system of the aisles. The scene looked like what it was, like a dying world fearful of death.

> Bobcat sticks around nervously in the hospital corridor until he hears Fossa is okay. The quality of his relief is romantic. Later on their affair is a light scandal that gives a frisson of transgression to the otherwise family-oriented, educationally minded show.
>
> Bobcat goes to a bar near the hospital where he meets a friend, a professor at the university. They get drunk. What a day Bobcat has had. The professor talks about students he is sleeping with. Bobcat is a true gentleman, or perhaps just kind of in his own head—he isn't having sex with anyone.

Once they're drunk, Bobcat is able to persuade his professor friend that they should test the strange dust from Fossa's shirt. Bobcat calls him Professor Gorilla. You would imagine that, as friends, they would be less formal. But for some people, for these people, their job is a big part of their identity. Like psychoanalysis, TV's big subjects are love and work.

At the lab, they examine the dust with special instruments. They are skeptical, then amazed, because it doesn't seem to be a material found on earth. Professor Gorilla wants to contact the government but Bobcat is like, hey wait a minute. He seems naturally suspicious of the government, which makes him more likable. He has up until now seemed pretty straitlaced, but now that his anti-state tendencies are coming out, he seems like he might be fun. In later episodes, his love for Fossa improves his character, motivating him to commit necessary crimes.

In this scene, he argues with Professor Gorilla that the town doesn't want the kind of attention that unexplained alien materials would bring. Foreshadowing a later plot line about an alien-worshipping cult, it's implied that the town has things to hide. Professor Gorilla agrees. It's implied that he is privately scheming. By episode four he and Bobcat will no longer be friends. Bobcat drives back to the hospital, head full of secrets, secrets.

"Sorry about your man," said the cashier at Target, from behind a mask and a Perspex screen.

For a second, Dog had no idea what she was talking about. The cashier pointed at Dog's chest. Dog was wearing his Moley Salamanders 2020 sweater. Only now that the cashier had drawn his attention to it did he remember that these proper nouns, Moley, Salamanders, 2020, used to convey meaning—a meaning that had structured his life up until just a couple of weeks ago.

"It's weird, but I don't care," said Dog.

The cashier could not make out the words, through the mask and the Perspex screen.

"I don't care!" yelled Dog, too loud.

A frisson of concern ran through the quiet checkout area. Ashamed of every aspect of himself, Dog took his little sack of necessary things and left the store.

But it was true: he didn't care. Looking back on his Moley days, it was as if he had spent months campaigning to have air conditioning installed in hell. Having now met the Devil, he had changed his mind. The entire slaughterhouse of the cosmos would have to be burned down instead, and a new life somehow built on its raw ashes. Was he turning into Bird? For the first time in weeks he wished for a thread to lead him away from the closed, foggy Fossa-world of sex, food and TV, stimulations ringing like church bells in his otherwise absolutely hollowed-out mind, back to the organized world.

Visiting hours are over by the time Bobcat arrives at the hospital, so he decides to get fictional Fossa's attention another way. He flashes a message in Morse code from the parking lot, and she comes outside in her hospital clothes. She still looks cute. She has the kind of radiantly Caucasian beauty that, like hard cash, is customarily accepted regardless of circumstance.

"I had a vision," she says. (This appears over and over in the episode recaps the entire first season, which is the only season, and so there are things we will never know.) "I saw something. It called to me. It has some kind of knowledge."

"I think it's from another planet," says Bobcat.

Two of Fossa's friends have come to see her too. The friends are Iguana (played by Fossa) and Dodo (played by a friend of Fossa's who died by accidental overdose a couple of years later). They're surprised to see Bobcat also there in the parking lot. Bobcat thought Fossa was there because she saw his Morse signal, but actually she was just there to meet her friends. Iguana is a beautiful black girl and Dodo is Peruvian. (The actor in real life was Mexican.) They are all at college together. Fossa is studying biology; Iguana is a double major in geology and ancient mythology, and Dodo is a computer science prodigy. They've seen Bobcat around on campus. Professor Gorilla is a friend of mine, he explains.

Every time Fossa sees herself onscreen is like the first time. Who is she? Me. I am what remains of her. A rebirth amid wasted time.

Back at the university lab, another scientist is working late, all alone. She finds the dust sample and the reading. She thinks the results must be a mistake. Maybe the equipment is broken. She runs the tests again. Yes, the dust is from another planet! She calls the FBI.

This is the pilot episode, and it's unusual in that it's only at this point in the story that we flashback to the ancient past. For the rest of the series, we begin at some point deep in ancient time, with an alien teaching a human something. The show's theory of history is that these lessons are the great leaps forward in human knowledge, unexplained by the historical record. Aliens teach humans how to work metal and describe the galactic neighborhood. In other ways they are not as smart as humans. They are confused by agriculture and animals. They consistently bring technology rather than a worldview. The show does not display any understanding that technology is the transformation of human social forces into objects. The show's theory of technology is that it arrives from beyond these social forces, i.e. from aliens.

The aliens never fully explain their relationship to humans, though they clearly feel obliged to transmit knowledge. It is left to Fossa and her friends to discover, over twelve episodes, that the aliens are emissaries of a wider project to familiarize humans with tech. Do the aliens intend to help us or to make use of us? The question is hard to answer, because throughout the show, aliens resist contact with Fossa and her friends. It is not until the season finale that they appear to Fossa and explain that they withdrew after humans had failed an important evolutionary test. They give few details, and the audience might well have anticipated a fuller account in the second season. There was never a second season. The actor who played Dodo overdosed and died in a hotel bathroom. The actor who played Fossa went on to star in a popular horror movie series, then had four kids with a Christian rock star. They were happily married and avoided the limelight. Jesus sometimes saves, but so many things can. Seeking self-destruction, Fossa combined her colleagues' two paths into half a life: she became addicted to painkillers and married a man whose overwhelming jealousy, masquerading as devotion, did not allow her to pursue an acting career. But this is only the first episode.

Dog got back to Fossa's from his shopping trip. He made a meal that could have been interpreted as either lunch or dinner back in the pre-pandemic days of the clock. Fossa didn't ask him where he had been. He found her lack of curiosity about him soothing, though he felt and ignored some subterranean agitation. She had not asked why he was still there, when he was planning to leave, how he felt about his friends' sudden death, or what was going on in his relationship. The kindness she seemed to want most from him was that of silence, and that was the kindness she gave him too: silence and her body, silence and her home, a silence that emanated from her despite the babble of the TV, which she had on constantly, to further discourage speech.

Every day the day became gradually less and less realistic. Each individual day felt increasingly crazy as sunset approached, and the mass of days grew as blurry and private as nights. Fossa's house was a barricaded town inhabited by hostile furniture. Dog slid off a chair onto the floor and crawled to Fossa over a stretch of deep-pile rug. She stroked his shoulders, he held her waist. Desire was a form of exhaustion, or it was the other way around. Their movements drew contours in the mess, the wash of time collapsing all around them. It was Tuesday or September or the end.

> Suddenly we are in the Nile Valley. This is before the pyramids. There is only the tidal delta caressing the earth into all forms of reception. There are people living in simple structures in the desert. They spend their time taking care of their children, searching for food and inventing games. They seem happy and lacking in curiosity. Part of the pleasure of the show is its depiction of prehistoric life. Everyone is happy and chill, with an occasional questing genius or intense Machiavellian schemer. Their existence is entirely focused around social life. No one leaves to

go to work or move to another town. Their cosmologies are full of personalities and animals.

The desert people think of the moon as an expressionless, shining bird, and the wind as the agitation of the ancestors. Only one of them is interested in understanding the world around them in a different way.

A weakness of the show is that it often depicts knowledge as emerging from individual intellects, rather than collective experience. This makes the show's prehistoric scenes feel unrealistic. Great leaps forward in human understanding most likely happened at moments of maximum concentrated collectivity. But that's hard to show on TV.

This special individual tries to get his friends to engage with how the stars move in a certain direction, that some are brighter than others and so on. He makes little diagrams in the sand with sticks and stones. Sometimes a child runs through and messes up a diagram, and he sighs and starts again.

The point of the show is that the stars are a guarantee of human intellectual development. Even if society gets completely broken down and fragmented and all knowledge is lost, there will still be the stars to show that the relation between pure chance and human time, with its meaningful births, deaths and seasons, is structured by a bigger field of moving parts. Even if class/race war and evil weather obliterate everything interesting, someone out there will be able to begin again, with the evening star that we call Venus or the unusually bright star in what we call the north. For better or worse, someone will observe that celestial movements are not random but happen in the strictest strangest order, and for better or worse the whole thing, the striving for art and knowledge, will begin again.

Real Fossa paused fictional Fossa and switched to a news site screening the president's daily press briefing. She was compelled to watch these several times a week. Dog hated them.

Pig was in the midst of his usual apocalypse stand-up routine. His being was transparent, a diaphanous thing he had thrown on against the elements. So the flow of his gleeful, terrified inanity was spiked with little rushes of fucked human essence, as well as punctuated by reporters asking questions without expecting answers, statements from a parallel world.

When Pig professed love of America, he sounded ironic. As his accidental irony hinted, every country is colonized by capital, which appears like a mirage, as a nation, and the mirage has a baby called national history, and we all have to live like that.

Fossa laughed because the president's freewheeling inner chaos, which had the texture of a child's devastated hopes of love, felt familiar and helped maintain her cherished half-disbelief in the plague. Dog too had the strong feeling of not being sure if life and death were real, but he did not want it. He asked Fossa to switch back to her TV show.

> One night the curious desert dweller is out looking at the stars, all alone. Two figures appear in the distance, walking towards him. He is a little afraid but waits. They come close and ask him what he is doing. He is surprised they speak in the language of his people, which his people just call language, but he answers. As far as he knows, language comes from the wind, and everyone speaks it. So much is still open, in the womb of the world: there has been no fall, no devil, no great authoritarian, no messianic arrival, no rupture, no departure, no serious break with the sensuous material of living. Perhaps disease and accident kill most people before thirty; perhaps they live three hundred years. Perhaps they die of hunger, or perhaps they experience their surroundings as more or less reliably abundant. So little is known. The show

could have done more with this wide blank field. The strangers move a few sticks and stones around.

"It's more like this," they tell him. "And in the winter it will look this way."

You can tell he's amazed. He's been working on this all alone for years, and now these strangers turn up and explain more than he could ever have dreamed.

He takes them back to his people, in some caves near a spring. They are gathered around a fire. Paintings of animals on rocks and trees dance in its unsteady light. The visitors have a great time. They seem pleased by the desert people's harmonious social life and creativity. They perform a dance, which, they explain, is a representation of the movements of the stars. The people are impressed by the dance, which is kind of fabulous: swirling, buoyant, prehistoric glam. At some point, the visitors start to lose their human shapes. Wings and claws sprout from their backs, from their hands and feet. Their skin loses its soft human texture and becomes scaly. The people look on in awe, but not fear. It is not yet known how the world is arranged. No one has yet tried to establish rules for how bodies behave. Multiple spirits move in the world as really existing things. With scaly hands and feet, the visitors slaughter a bird and use its blood to draw on the rock. They draw a map of the constellations. They point out the planet they come from. They promise that everyone will eventually visit there, and then they leave.

Dog was suddenly, profoundly homesick for Bird.

Real-life Fossa's thoughts were folded deeper in her past.

"I used to be so beautiful," she said.

Fossa was still beautiful, but Dog said nothing. He guiltily experienced his own silence as sadistic, but Fossa didn't notice; all her attention was on the image of her younger self, onscreen.

An FBI guy has arrived in town, wanting to speak to the fictional Fossa, who hides out at Iguana's place with Dodo. They call Bobcat—perhaps he will know what to do.

"This is the first episode," Dog said.

"Yeah."

"We're starting from the beginning again?"

"There's only one season," said Fossa.

MAY

Explaining to the Aliens

It was a time of signs and wonders, though none of them were good. Bird received a check for $1200 from the US government. President Pig had worked a miracle. He had shown that money could be made to flow directly from the godhead. Thanks to this, it still seemed possible for him to win a second term, despite the sirens, bereavements, panics, corpses.

If only the collapse of the Moley Salamanders campaign and the arrival of the aliens hadn't rendered the savage compromises of the Democrat Party fully historically redundant, they could have been gaining ground right now. They were hollowed out, waiting for whatever winds of history to take them like a sail. Pig had made himself briefly synonymous with relief. He had broken open the bank of his body, his second body, the pink ceramic bubble in which he stored repressed memories of childhood alongside wild, thrashing thoughts harvested directly from the mind of capital.

This latter was an atavistic world-mind, the aliens explained, left over from an exploded galactic civilization that had done something weird and ontologically illegal with time. The dissemination of this ugly tendency throughout all of space/time, said the aliens, was referred to in their culture with a semantic unit exactly equivalent to *pandemic*. Beyond that, sadly, almost nothing about the means and organization of the aliens' language could yet be conveyed in human language. To bridge the culture gap, the aliens instated a system resembling jury duty and known informally as Explaining to the Aliens, interviewing selected humans one by one.

The aliens came from a system with two suns, in a configuration as unlikely and impossibly perfect as that which produced life on Earth. They had no intellectual sense of number, which for them was experienced sensorily. They had arts, but no architecture—in fact, they considered architecture immoral, shocking, and it caused them some pain on Earth. They had similar relational concepts approximating to love and sex, but no experience with property or generational inheritance.

Humanity had meekly submitted itself as an object of study. The aliens constantly secreted some kind of ultra-attractive pheromone that put them out of the remit of politics, much further even than love.

*

Pandemic border regulations did not permit Bird to return directly home. No one knew exactly what the rules were. Borders had become zany and negotiable, like raw frontier. There was a possible route back via a two-week quarantine in Mexico.

Once she had decided to leave, it was as if she could have left all along. In purgatorial time, like insurrectionary time, the present is a mirage of punishment hiding an open door. The aliens had re-birthed her from her family. It seemed that, without knowing, this was what she had come back to England to do. She did not know what else the aliens had done since they changed her life. She had not yet been called up to Explain. Like Alpaca, she was no longer interested in the news. She wrote him a postcard, a bland declaration of gratitude and friendship that would arrive after she had safely departed.

You could end things just as easily as you began them, without thinking. There was no resistance to events in the fabric of time.

The principle of trees followed Bird around like the moon follows a car. In London, oaks, chestnuts and willows remembered old managements of land. She admired them more in Mexico City: cypress, ficus, jacaranda, willow, and others she didn't have names for. They lined the streets with photosynthetic possibility. There was a human-smelling pollen. It was still possible to be born.

Her friend Capybara showed her around the pandemic-shuttered city as if guiding her around an archeological site, pointing out the various absences: the sloping public surfaces once enjoyed by skaters, the parks and squares where tourists and addicts congregated long ago, the bars where art students used to get wasted. So much had been temporarily abolished.

From Capybara's rooftop Bird saw how fast the city succumbed to sunset. The altitude took her breath. With an outstretched hand, Capybara pointed out districts and directions, giving a physical body to a place that would otherwise have vanished in Bird's senses as no more than a dream way-station en route back to her life. A stream of alien vehicles passed by in silhouette before the fast-setting sun, coming in and out of Havana.

*

In New York City, the radio in the taxi blared alien news.

V

The right had turned against them now that they were Cuba-aligned. Bird laughed out loud.

The air was spiked with pollen from the sycamores and maples on her street. Her nose and eyes streamed behind her mask as she opened her front door with the keys she had kept with her.

It was two days before the day deeply stained through space/time by the murder of George Floyd. It was five days before the Third Precinct in Minneapolis was set on fire.

On that day, cops stuffed the weapons and restraints of their trade into trash bags and hastily evacuated the scene of domination. So little like it had been seen before. The alien collective mind had suffered from the introduction of the concept of prison, but it was deeply healed by riot and even gained new strength. Through social influence, like the virus, unrest immediately spread to New York City. Looters swept through SoHo, temporarily annihilating the commodity form. It was the beginning of the world.

Feeling seeped back into Bird's numbed-out soul as she remembered the possibility of an active, transformative practice of mourning. Light of the world! She was home. The dead stayed dead, but the living not yet—riot was the shining overlap of these two spectacular facts.

*

Thank you for your support of our understanding efforts.

    Did I have a choice?

Yes and no. The word is glued to people. What's yours?

    Fossa.

We learn from you. What are you from?

    I was born in the Bronx, New York.

We know the place—ocean sediments. Are words related to the ancient water? We know that objects also have the shape of a frame. The brain is the main part of speech we know.

    There was water there a very long time ago. Geologists call it the Iapetan Ocean, but there was no one to call it anything at the time.

Does the name cause what you call death?

    No. Maybe. A name makes it seem like

something was born and died. But it was just planetary churn, making space and taking it away. Only a creature can be born. That's our loss.

We know erosion sanded down the catastrophic forms. The rough resistance line seems to be important because the geological years are as numerous as the human epidermal nerve endings. So we can imagine how much touch means to you. What do you touch?

There was a man around not so long ago—I'm not sure, but he must have been real because I sent him away. I forget my body is about me. I forget the handle of the skillet gets too hot to touch directly. My objects haunt me. I bought all this? All day I move my things around. Folds and corners in the body—I'm in constant contact with myself. It depends on what and who you think of as having an inner life. I wasn't, when I was cast as a beautiful girl. Though if you're black there's always the shadow of sedition, which isn't nothing.

Is black the color of the rocks multiplied by tides, who are sand?

> No, no. I don't know where to begin.

We know that fire is orange, yellow, and blue, and these are only colors associated with burning that occur in the eye broken off from the world. But why do people burn buildings?

> Because the police killed a man.

In Los Angeles, 1992?

> That time they only almost killed him. But there are always others killed elsewhere or already dead or living way too close to dying. The spectacle of harm, that's just what everyone can see, not the full extent of harm. It's not only about death or killing. It's the new angle you can see world horror from.

You were there, we know.

> What can I say about '92? I remember crying in a parking lot, but I didn't care that the world was ending. Burn it all down.

Fire?

Yes, burn it all down. I live a quiet life, but I still believe that.

We track the wet bags of the lungs—they record the inner world container. Police are mobile prison and control the movement of bags, moving bags to stillness with poison, electricity, popular weapons or body forces, but why?

Why? This is a prison world, and so there are police.

There is a high removal rate on this planet. We are surprised by the high degree of abstraction of exchange. There was nothing like money in the chemical composition.

Police exist to make property stay property. They expect respect for that— thousands of evil daddies in every city. They kill openly and lie non-stop. Ask anyone. If they don't have weapons, they kill with their feet, knees, hands. They kill children at play. And so on.

The growth of carbon dioxide is driven by the movement of the internal organs and transformed by oxygen. Please make sure.

That's right, yes.

But you feel nothing about this?

> Almost nothing.

Who named the dead ocean?

> You're lucky that Iguana got me into this. She was a fiction—I embodied her, so we're still close. I played her on TV, and she was a good student. Iapetus held up the western part of the sky. He was the god of mortality.

Police?

> No. In myths there are no police. Some people think Chronos, the god of time, was also one of Iapetus's brothers. They all helped him castrate their father.

Is this the beginning of the harmful effects of the celestial planet?

> Yes, if you look at it from Chronos's point of view, holding a bloody sickle in his hand, mutilating his father to give him his first period and inaugurate time. Then time ovulated coinage, and that was how secular death was born.

We almost die like you. But we have nothing resembling the immortality of finances, the undead material, capital. Your society networked substance. It was not in the original materials.

> When I look at the situation from your point of view, I feel sorrow.

What is sorrow?

> It's something like emptiness plus unease.

Before fire?

> If you believe what these people say about themselves, before the discovery of fire there was no eagle to eat Prometheus's liver every night— no romance, basically, no concept of forever. The whole scheme of the human had to begin by making punishment immortal.

Before the fire in Minneapolis?

> Before that there was nothing at all, since Ferguson.

We put limestone and shale. World-time ate rhyolite, granite and volcanic tuff. We planted metamorphic sediments via glacial transport. A certain type of land grew. Like your word, unease. We share your power of making a mistake.

> You did all that? Some people will be disappointed. Believers in a geological god.

We do not want to give up. It is not difficult to understand. The chaos of the world prepares beautiful arrangements such as the chaos mirror as a tool for ordering. It's better if you let the words. We are moved to carbon by you. To us you speak as many. Microbes, generations.

> The problem is there is so much more world than I can explain. But not infinitely, because I have told you some of it.

VI JUNE

OR THE END

Or The End

Everything had become subject to death, and therefore alive. So machines and networks were as alive as ideas and the ghosts of the past were, if you believed in them—all beliefs were alive now. That is to say it was all dying. The cities were dying, the insects en masse, the restaurant industry, the ice sheets, the gender regime. Democracy was dying—then again, it had never fully been born. But people who really had been born were also dying, away from those who could help them die. So there was a spiritual restlessness always in the air.

In this phase of maximum life, the shadow of death hung over everything. This death was not a judgment, out of which a religion and therefore a routine could have been made. It was just a fact always disappearing around the corner. It was what had happened because the living world had been brutalized and abstracted. Life/death in the form of a virus rebelled against its objectification as capitalist value. In a system that perversely generated its force from rebellion against it, that had never meant much before, but now the steady presence of the aliens gave rebellion a living body, an outer skin.

The incomprehensible covid death toll spread out into a kind of miasma, present as fog at the awful periphery, sometimes drifting into the raw center. An aunt in Miami who Bird hadn't seen for years, a former colleague, a neighbor. No one she knew well enough to mourn deeply, but she felt the accumulation of absences. The people closest to her survived or avoided the disease, but the weave of being sagged with gaps.

Though the state was always making these holes, through its Plutonic capture of sex and death, the shared world kept rolling through them like a handful of dice, powered by the mechanism of infinite chance. Without the aliens, history could have unfolded differently. With material and even defensive military support from the alien base in Cuba, the riots grew to world-changing proportions. Love of aliens melted fascist sympathies, eroding the social base of reaction.

The riots became a daily practice. Bird was reunited with the city and her friends. She had returned to New York during a local phase of the affirmation of life. A period of total introversion had flowered instantly into maximum social activity, *the* maximum social activity: revolution.

For Bird, hungry for and uncertain of others, it was medicinal and magical. Every day she saw a hundred new signs that no world was too good to be destroyed and renewed by the people it was made up of. Every day she saw a thousand new signs that a world that thought itself too good to be destroyed and renewed was bound to death and the secularization of death.

The riots made the world new, and sadness is always old, so in that brand new summer, in the liquid return of feeling, Bird forgot to dwell on her losses. The losses themselves were healed by the novelty of being with others, and not only that, but seeing police cars burn, and not only that. Her soul rushed toward the riot. She had no opinion about her fate. The wheel of fortune spun wildly; the future was infinitely open.

Bird and her friends received six hundred dollar unemployment checks every week. They had so much time for themselves and each other. They had so much time for the uprising.

Precincts burned in all five boroughs. Cops quit in their hundreds, and some immediately went down to one of the people's encampments that had sprung up around the city, to confess their sins and ask for the people's forgiveness. Workers, first at Trader Joe's, then all the major grocery store chains, refused to take payment for goods: THE COMMODITY FORM IS NON-CONSENSUAL, read a banner draped over the Whole Foods on East Houston. At citywide #MeToo meetings, workers of all kinds gathered to describe the ways they had been harmed, humiliated and degraded by bosses.

The state governor Anteater Cormorant cut off supply chains to the city, hoping to starve the riot. His children publicly denounced him, but it wasn't even necessary: a group of revolutionary truckers ignored the order and drove deliveries of food and medicine through checkpoints at full speed. Supplies flowed in from the aliens' headquarters in Cuba via the port, which was controlled by the riot.

Bird did not know where Dog was, and she did not try to find out. He was living in his brother's basement in Washington Heights. Though they thought of each other, they made no attempts to get in touch, as if held apart by an unknown physical law. One night, chance almost brought them together in front of a looted Apple store, but Dog left to watch Pig Tower burn five minutes before Bird arrived. Later, neither regretted how long it had taken them to run into each other: chance was just destiny dressed in everyday clothes.

Skirmishes continued throughout the city, led by a hardcore NYPD contingent who would not give up even in the face of the riot's courage, alien support and vastly superior numbers. By mid-June, everyone had grown expert in barricades, and even after the police retreated to Staten Island, the people kept inland stretches of barricade intact. These remainders resembled public sculptures whose form fluctuated daily as people took parts away and added others. It became customary to refer to the network of friends and associates who held barricades according to a rotating, ever-evolving schedule as the people's army. It was a joke because military discipline was absent: there were no rules, though behavior was endlessly discussed; there were no uniforms, though you could detect unspoken dress codes, and no fixed leaders, though some were listened to more than others. The term *army* nevertheless caused consternation in the media; infographics and videos were shared explaining that the movement was non-hierarchical and operated according to discussion and consent. But perhaps the unfortunate term was why Governor Cormorant finally colluded with the president in allowing the National Guard to enter the city. In scenes broadcast internationally over and over for months after, a National

Guard unit met with a contingent of protestors on the George Washington Bridge, and there they kneeled with the people. They burned the bridge immediately after, as a precaution against further invasion. This event appeared immediately in that night's revolutionary chants, as shamefully simple as love songs, symbolizing a complete break with the past. What would be done with those who clung to this abolished past? Without universal law, each would follow their own fate. In some neighborhoods they held trials and in others there were passionate murders. The problem of revolutionary tyranny melted into the discovery of each other. It was unreal. It was a dream.

A public discussion on the NYPD budget outside City Hall began what no one knew then would be a nine-month public debate about what the form of the new city commune would be—at first an argument, then self-consciously evoking a new democratic form, then becoming the complicated reality of this image. The discussion spanned many subjects and continued to be referred to as City Hall. City Hall itself had been torched during a pitched battle between the NYPD and the people. The charred, skeletal remains of the building, still partly enclosed in stone walls, stood as an inverse image of administration. It served as an open-air office: politicians converted to the riot, organizers and whoever was there that day all busied themselves with running the city, primarily tasks of coordination. Shorn of its pre-riot abstractions, the business of everyday life was enacted with surprising efficiency. Like a baby, the city needed constant care and tending but was fundamentally possessed of its own will to live.

During the month of June, all prisoners were officially released, medical debt was cancelled, rent was abolished and billions of dollars of public money was given to mutual aid groups around the city. These groups had begun to organize themselves into neighborhood zones with rotating representatives at City Hall. Inner allegiances and conflicts meant the groups took different, sometimes non-complementary shapes: naturally the structure of revolutionary administration of Brownsville looked different than that of Astoria or Crown Heights, according to the class and race composition of each neighborhood. Though it was widely acknowledged that these differences had to be lived with before they could be bridged, city bureaucrats sympathetic to the revolution did their best to help mediate. The evacuated shell of the state was retrofitted to perform new, pro-social functions. At times the conflict among different factions threatened to break the revolution apart, and only the presence of a shared external enemy and the careful interventions of the aliens kept the people of New York City focused on the task of undoing and remaking. It was the same all over the country: the old forms died in fits and starts, and the new forms were arduously and ecstatically born.

Given all this, it was decided that time had to be made for general and spiritual questions at City Hall. This decision itself took two full days, and for some reason no one could later remember most of this time was spent arguing about if individual freedom had to mean chaos and/or isolation. Some people argued that this association was a fantasy or fear born from the pain of childhood. Others maintained that the concept of the individual was a foundational flaw of capitalist society and had to be overcome. They were criticized for their lack of realism. But did the link between the individual and the collective, whatever it was, represent a practical hard limit on freedom, or did it demand a change in desire?

Although no final conclusions could be drawn, the discussion helped a lot of people think through their attachment to the war machine and the police. It was as if everyone there had begun a relationship with each other. Inevitably there was both pleasure and pain. But in the early days, in the thrill of victory, it was easier to focus on pleasure.

Bird was lucky to be there on the day that the people entered Rikers and liberated the prison. Smashing open locks and breaking down doors, thousands roamed freely through the architecture of previous misery, singing, crying, laughing, embracing, as the few remaining guards fled or faced the rough justice of the crowd. Though two guards, known sadists, died that day, retribution was far less severe than Bird would have imagined. The crowd wanted relief from suffering and the happiness of a new future much more than they wanted revenge. A delegation of until-now-incarcerated people gathered and immediately found an audience with the aliens, who had been waiting all their lives, they said, to hear from them. Differences between human and alien language were gradually becoming less unwieldy, though teams of linguists, translators and poets had to work day and night to understand alien speech. The alien language had no subjects or objects. It had no possessive pronouns. It had no verb tenses to indicate time.

Three days after the liberation of Rikers, a giant sinkhole opened beneath it and it was swallowed by the Earth. Within days, its former existence began to sound like a lurid myth, even to the people who had once lived and worked there.

Across all forms—music, memes, etc—artists strove to express the weird feeling of being broken open into a new collective life. In the individual body, the revolution felt as if the hands and feet had snapped off at the end of the arms and legs, the head too had hinged perfectly and cleanly from the neck, and it turned out that the body was just brimming with a universal light that now radiated outwards. As if exhausted by something like sex, you both could and could not walk around like that because so sincerely focused on an inner satisfaction/longing.

There was the long Monday when a delegation from the decommissioning team at Indian Point, the nuclear power station just north of the city, arrived to share some urgent concerns. That day, though full of logistical and practical questions, was strangely emotional. Everyone felt moved and scared by the absolute reality of their situation. There was momentary harmony within the congress. It was decided, amid sentimental speeches, that the budget and oversight for the decommissioning process would be offered to the indigenous congress that was happening simultaneously on Long Island.

The break in constant argument was short. Liberal holdouts among the representatives from the mutual aid zones of Park Slope and the Upper West Side felt that the handover was irresponsible and premature—and they made their feelings clear. The UWS representatives took the humiliating step of officially declaring their loyalty to Anteater Cormorant. It was too late: everyone believed the recent rumor that he had crossed the border into Canada and was hiding out with other remnants of the American political establishment while he waited to see what would unfold. The Upper West Side's allegiances only emphasized the obvious fact that the bourgeois neighborhoods were weak links in defending the city from the cops and assorted armed reactionaries who still, though with declining courage, fought to turn back the tide of transformation.

The more advanced mutual aid zones gave their liberals non-representative honorary or harmless positions such as grocery co-ordination or community exercise, and thus placated, most of them stayed more-or-less loyal to the revolution. Some of the wealthiest in the city were strangely reluctant to leave, considering they had many places to go, but the helipads of Manhattan were often frequented by ageless vampires sneaking a last goodbye glimpse of the skyline, a surreal image of labor that they mistook for the victory of their greed.

Collective kitchens set up during the most intense period of street fighting were made permanent. Empty housing was commandeered and put to immediate use. Police stations were wrecked and, later, turned into museums of the police. Parents and teachers visited with small children and took pleasure in explaining cops in emphatic past tense, as if the whole business of policing had ended years ago. On the whole, behaviors once categorized as crime had reduced sharply, though those behaviors that had never fully been accommodated into the logic of crime—sexual violence, domestic abuse—continued wherever they were entrenched in psyches, communities and relationships. Emboldened by the general upheaval, however, the victims were more likely than in pre-revolutionary times to extricate themselves from intimate bondage. They went out into the streets where they found, in many cases, support from the various therapeutic, somatic and psychoanalytic groups of all kinds that had sprung up during the revolution, held outdoors in parks and empty lots.

The streets teemed with people day and night; it was as if no one ever went indoors. The burned-out blocks of SoHo and Chinatown, where NYPD had at one point drone-bombed buildings in their effort to regain control, were razed to the ground and converted into orchards. Transplanted from elsewhere, the trees took root and grew astonishingly fast. Time had thickened; the uprising had changed the texture of time, giving each minute new depth. Each minute shone like ocean at the surface. From each minute, multiple possible outcomes, reactions and phrases previously locked up in the quanta of capital folded out, expanding the surface area of time.

Fruit sprang from trees grown so tall they leaned

into the high windows of buildings and canopied the blocks of Lower Manhattan. People browsed liberated commodities in the outdoor markets, on sidewalks that now resembled a forest floor. Similarly, as small clusters of people on folding chairs in empty lots discussed childhood, thankless work and lost love in soft voices, the buried wounds of the past came up for air, aping a plant's stubborn sunward journey through layers of earth that helped and hindered like (the concept of) a mother. Fertilized by the new abundance of time, past pain unfurled leaves on which were written a glowing scripture of renewed life. The letters curled and blurred and fell away from each other. They resembled the alien alphabet: as June drew to a close, the poets and linguists finally made the happy discovery that the alien slime trails previously mistaken for excretions had been, all along, an interpretable orthography. At last there was the possibility of a shared language.

Reaching up to judge the ripeness of an apple growing on Broadway, Bird glimpsed Dog through the foliage of the tree. His face struck her like the ongoing shock of being able to read. You know how that shock can inspire a kind of commitment, if you have been with me this long. Recognizing him, her body acknowledged that expericnce accumulated in it. Experience had not in fact leaked away through the many holes they had made in their love.

Half-obliterated by plague then resurrected by riot, Dog and Bird went to find out what was still intact between them, as the people declared the New York Commune from the ruins of City Hall.

OR THE END

Hannah Black
Tuesday or September or the End

Edited by Anika Sabin
Copyedit by Logan Becker

Interior design by Erica Bech
Cover design by Sacha Lo
Design Assistance by David Lindsay

Published by Capricious

145 Elizabeth Street
New York, NY 10012

ISBN 978-1-7346562-3-7

© 2022 All rights reserved. Capricious Publishing as an entity of Capricious Foundation and Hannah Black.